T0078387

HURRICANE ADA
and the
WINDS OF CHANGE

MARKEITH AND IRMA PORTER

WESTBOW
PRESS®
A DIVISION OF THOMAS NELSON
& ZONDERVAN

WestBow Press books may be ordered through booksellers or by contacting:

WestBow Press
A Division of Thomas Nelson & Zondervan
1663 Liberty Drive
Bloomington, IN 47403
www.westbowpress.com
844-714-3454

Scripture taken from the King James Version of the Bible.

ISBN: 978-1-6642-1743-0 (sc)
ISBN: 978-1-6642-1795-9 (e)

Library of Congress Control Number: 2020926014

Print information available on the last page.

WestBow Press rev. date: 01/13/2021

This book is dedicated to our Lord and Savior. With every move I make, I hope I have my Lord's favor, because without him, I am nothing. Peter denied him three time before the rooster crowed. I want to acknowledge his presence in my life.

I also dedicate this book to all the beautiful women who have inspired me. My wife, Irma, is a hurricane in her own right. My big sister, Sandra, is as strong as any man and can hold her own against anyone. She is definitely an Ada. My mother is a fast learner. As a child, she taught me to learn lessons from others. You do not have to go through the same issues as others if you use your head.

HURRICANE ADA AND THE WINDS OF CHANGE

My father was a proud man. Some would say too prideful. He was a champion cricket player for the village. It was great watching him play for he was the best. He could hit the ball so far that it would travel to the edge of the jungle, where no one could find it. We would laugh and make jokes. "Where is the ball? You cannot find it. It is lost in the jungle."

My brother was timid as a boy. My father would chastise him for not being a man. He would say thing like "You lazy boy, why do you not hunt with the rest of the young men? Instead, you hang around your mother too much." My older brother had confidence. It was not a manly confidence as my father portrayed but confidence nevertheless. He did not take on tasks that were larger than he was. He would play cricket like my father but was never that good at the game. He thought he was better than he was. He could catch pretty well but was never a good slugger. My father would be embarrassed at his effort. He would close his eyes and hide his face when my brother batted.

My older brother would antagonize the antelope in the fields. He would play silly games with the wild animals. He would often make them scatter, which caused stampedes of farmers' crops. This would cause hate and discontent from the neighbors. The neighbors wanted to hang him by his feet and whip him senseless to make him stop.

My younger brother was much like my father. He would follow him around, stating everything little thing my father world say, such as "You goofball." That was my father's way of calling us silly. But calling us silly meant calling himself silly because we all emulated our father.

My name is Adah, meaning "beautiful ornament," but most call me Ada, meaning "oldest sister." As oldest sister, I would fish the river. I was quite good at it too. This would be my only praise from my father because he loved fish. I would feed the entire family and help clean and cook the fish. My father would thank our Holy Father, and then he would thank me for my hard work. This made me happy.

Carrying water was one of my tasks as a girl. This I hated. My father and mother would tell me to go fetch some water from the river. This was dangerous, but we did it. Most of the time, it was my mother and I. We would talk and talk about becoming a woman and performing women things. My mother was a kind woman, and she taught me the art of healing. She taught that the plants are all we need to survive. As a girl one, of my jobs was feeding the animals: the pigs, the goats, the chickens, and the cows. Each morning, I woke to do this mundane task. I felt like dying inside. My brothers would hunt and work the fields. They would be with my father most of the day as I wanted. I did not like my mother's chores and wanted to be seen as the best. And the best is not found feeding chickens.

My dad treated my brothers with great admiration. They would follow him even though my oldest brother hated it. He followed because that is what boys do. They follow in the footsteps of their fathers. My father at church would tell everyone about their conquest for the week. For instance, if my oldest brother caught a highflyer in cricket, that would be the top topic of conversation. I would ask my father if I could play cricket, but he would laugh and say, "It is not for girls." I would question his thinking and say, "Why not for girls?" This would infuriate him beyond belief. He would tell me to leave and go sit with my mother.

Ada, always the gregarious one, wanted to hunt with her brother. Even against her father's wishes, the oldest brother would let Ada follow along. She was tough, and she could hold her own against any man. She would tell her brother, "Let me shoot the bow. I can do it." She was quite handy with the bow and arrow. At fifty yards, she was an outstanding shot, even with a moving target. Her father at fifteen years old went hunting with his dad. A lion chased, and he froze, not earning an arrow scar in the face. His father was upset. He called my father a coward. My father did not want much to do with Grandpa after those mean words.

Three bells tolled from the church Ada and her family attended regularly. This happened to be a sermon on talents. The father of the church told the story of the landlord who had three servants. To each he gave talents, in accordance with their ability. One servant he gave five talents, another he gave two talents, and another he gave one talent.

The servant with five talents went out and made five more talents, which equaled ten. The servant he gave two talents to went out and made two more talents, which equaled four. These servants made the landlord very happy. The one servant he gave one talent to went out and buried his talent, wasting any profit on the landlord's talent. The servant with one talent told the landlord he knew him to be a hard man, reaping where he did not sow. "I buried the talent. I did not want to lose what you had given freely." He wasted his talent. "He did not try, and that is not what I will do with my talent," stated Ada. "I will at least try to change things."

Ada, looking for her father's approval, went fishing one morning. On her way, she looked over the tall grass and saw a young male lion stalking her brother near the river. He had gone to fetch water for their mother. Ada dropped her fishing pole and net and ran back to the house to get her father's bow and arrow. She returned just in time as the young lion was on the attack. Ada was quite fast. Young and gifted with extra talent, she killed the lion with one shot. A neighbor saw this remarkable feat and told the whole village. They praised her with song and a feast for kings. They danced all night. Her father grew angrier by the minute. He who had been a champion cricket player had no such praise. He stated, "A daughter should never overrun her father."

Ada's father, upset with her about killing the lion, sent her brother hunting. He knew Ada would want to tag along. He knew her character, and he hated it. He egregiously talked to slave traders and told them to snatch his daughter up and leave her brother behind. The slave traders took both into custody and locked them up in chains. The dad heard of this and went off to find the captain of the *USS Deliverance* to ask him to let his son go. The captain told him to pay $100 to get him released. The father did not have the money.

The father went to several people in the village to obtain the money for his son. He could not raise the money before the *USS Deliverance* set sail.

The night before the ships set sail, the *USS Deliverance* and the *USS Port Royal* captains were in disagreement as to taking the two young people into slavery. They said, "Let them grow a bit." One of the captains said, "The young girl, Ada, must be more trouble than she is worth. Her own father sold her into slavery."

The next day, the ships set sail for America. The ships were out at sea when the brother told his sister he would escape. She told him, "Where will you go? Do not leave me. We are miles from land."

The brother stated, "Freedom or death is my quest. Tell Father and Mother that I love them." He also told her he would be with her regardless of the outcome.

The older brother faked seasickness. One of the guards came over to assist and let him go topside for a moment. He hit the guard with his chains and ran to the opening to go topside. He was immediately trapped by the ship's crew. One said, "Boy, easy does it. We don't want to hurt you, but we will if we have to."

Just then, his whole life flashed in front of him, from the time he saw his sister born until the time his sister killed the lion. He said a prayer and jumped to his death.

All the captain said was "He was fine cargo. We may have lost $100 on that one."

The captain, wanting to know what his cargo was worth, went into the cargo bay and surveyed the people he had above. He saw Ada, young and beautiful but powerful looking, with muscles in her cheekbones. She had strong-looking legs. The captain ordered the men to take her to his stateroom, where he attempted to have relations with the young girl. She put up a fight. The captain sent her away, putting her in solitary confinement for three days.

Ada arrived into a new world in South Carolina. She got sold at auction and fetched a healthy price. One man stated, "She will do wonders in the fields." The auctioneer stated, "Ada, now close to seventeen, works the fields at the plantation. She works better than any man."

Recognizing that she would only get back to where she came from by being free, her plan was to work hard enough to earn her freedom. When one man would carry one bale of cotton, she would carry two. The overseer saw this and began to talk to the owner. He said, "The girl Ada is a hard worker. Maybe you should take her into the house to replace Ida. Ida is getting up in age. She will not be here for that much longer."

Ada was popular in the village. She would tell amazing stories of the village she came from. She told the story of a black mamba snake that killed three people before he was caught. With all the people in the village, it took a woman to capture the snake by setting a trap of a rat and a box. The snake was killed, and life went on.

She told the story of a herd of elephants trampling through the fields of vegetables and eating everything in sight. When the villagers tried to scare them away, they scared them in the direction of the village and many of the huts were destroyed. The village learned a valuable lesson from that incident.

She told the story of a group of red-bottom baboons. A family came home to a family of red-bottom baboons. They tried to scare the baboons away, but they would not leave. They hissed and hawed until the family felt it was time to move on. It took two days before the baboons left the hut to go back the valley they came from.

Ada was reluctant to leave the fields. She had become so comfortable with fields that it was hard to go to the big house. She could barely speak English. She knew it would be difficult to learn, so she went at the request that the master taught her English. The master agreed. He told his daughter to make sure Ada had a good understanding of the English language. Ada was an excellent student, and she kept the house up to standard. She would keep the linens and clothes bright white. She would be trusted to get supplies from the local store. They knew her by name. She had gained the town's trust. Ada delved into remedies from the plants around her. She could cure most any illness, such as constipation. She could cure diarrhea. She had remedies for headaches. A massage was given for back pain. She got so good at the remedies that the people in the village called her a witch doctor. Nevertheless, she was so good the other plantation workers would come for one of her cures.

The master of the house fell sick and called for the local doctor. The doctor told him to stay off his feet for a week. He was with an illness that would eventually cause him to die. It was a fatal illness. He was with fever, and the doctor's medicine did not work. His daughter asked him to use Ada.

He said, "Ada is for the slaves, not for us civilized folks."

His daughter said, "Give Ada a chance, and if she cures you, you could award her with her freedom."

"There you go talking about freedom for slaves again. I am sick, and all you can do is kill me with your language."

The master called for the doctor again, and the doctor told him he had taken a turn for the worse. "You might want to make peace with your maker."

The daughter told him to give Ada a chance.

He stated, "Over my dead body."

The daughter said, "It will be over your dead body soon."

The master relented and gave Ada a chance to cure him. Ada worked tirelessly to get him back on his feet.

After two weeks of remedies and cures, she got him to sit up. After a month, he was walking gingerly. After two months, he was back barking orders to the slaves. He was forever grateful to Ada. But not enough to grant her freedom. She was too valuable. The master started taking on other plantation workers' sicknesses for payment. The masters of other plantations would pay for Ada's services.

Word got around that Ada was playing doctor and taking money from the local doctor. A group of men concerned about the town's reputation got together to talk with the master and said Ada had got to stop helping folks. She was taking money from their local doctor. The master said, "If the local doctor cannot hold his own against a slave girl with no training, then he is the problem, not Ada."

A worker from another plantation came to see the would-be witch doctor and found an old friend from the village in Africa. She immediately recognized Ada because Ada was a hero in the village. She asked Ada, "What happened to your brother? He disappeared around the same time you did. We heard your father sold you to slavery."

Ada said, "What?"

"Your father sold you to slavery."

"Then my father killed my oldest brother. He jumped from the ship we were on to his death. He could not stand being in chains. My father is a dead man," Ada claimed.

The worker received Ada's care, and she returned to her own plantation.

Ada immediately started her campaign to leave the plantation. She asked the master for her freedom, and he told her she had a good life. "What is making you want to leave?"

Master could not understand how Ada could want to leave her life on the plantation. In his thought process, Ada had it better than most. How could she want her freedom?

Ada announced, "Freedom is not something you should have to give me. I earned freedom at my God-given birth. It is a right, not a privilege. You yourself would have it no other way. Why should I not have the same?"

The master's daughter fell ill from the same sickness her father had had. The master told Ada, "If you cure her, you can have your freedom."

Ada worked tirelessly. She worked even to the expense of her own family. She had to get back to the village to kill her father for the death of her brother.

Ada saved the master's daughter. It took about two months, the same as for her father.

Ada married after some time a man who was happy-go-lucky. The man was known for his ability to carry large bales of cotton. He told her she was beautiful. Ada did not know how to respond. She told him, "Be gone with your mess. I am ugly. My father said so. He said the oldest sister is always the ugliest."

The man said, "Your face is strong. You have a scar because someone hurt you."

She said, "The scar is not because someone hurt me. The scar represents me coming of age and killing a young lion that was about to kill my brother."

"So Ada, you are a hero. In Swahili, that is *shujaa*."

Ada immediately took a voyage back to her village in Africa. With every breath, she thought about how she would kill her father.

After a two-month voyage, she arrived in Africa. She went to her village. Her father did not recognize her, and he was ashamed. The father, after learning his daughter was home, killed the fattest calf, and the whole village celebrated. Ada was looking for a time to be alone with her father, but it took days.

Her father was in a hut. She walked in and pulled out her pistol, and her father saw.

He told her she should pull the trigger. "I ordered you sold into slavery because I was jealous. You killed a lion when I choked up. I de facto killed my son. You see, Ada, you are like a hurricane. You blow away everything in your path to change the landscape. You have changed everyone's thinking regarding the place for a woman. You have caused the winds to shift in the direction of the women, and I cannot support that as a man. You see, I deserve to die."

Ada cocked the pistol before she pulled the trigger. The three bells tolled from the church. She remembered the sermon on the five talents. She identified with the servant who had five talents and turned those five talents into five more talents. If she pulled the trigger, she would be like the man with one talent. He buried his one talent, and to her, if she pulled the trigger, she would waste her talent. This was below Ada's character.

Ada did not pull the trigger. She in fact forgave her father because her Father in heaven had forgiven her.

Ada found common ground with her father even with her brother's death. Ada was unapologetic when it came to her attitude toward women. She believed her father had to change, and he soon began to understand that a woman can accomplish many of the same tasks as men.

THE END.

ABOUT THE AUTHOR

Markeith Porter is a military veteran that has had a extensive career in the US Navy. The adventures to numerous locations around the world have given me a excellent assessment of the character of people in their natural habitat. Irma is nurse that cares for everyone. Even those that would shun her care. She is a woman with a heart of gold and that perspective need to herd around the world

Printed in the United States
By Bookmasters